Story and Illustrations
By Michael Roach

Xlibris Book Publishing

To order additional copies of this book, contact:
Xlibris
844-714-8691
www.Xlibris.com
Orders@Xlibris.com

ISBN: 979-8-3694-0420-1 (sc)
ISBN: 979-8-3694-0740-0 (hc)
ISBN: 979-8-3694-0419-5 (e)

Library of Congress Control Number: 2023913879

Print information available on the last page

Rev. date: 09/14/2023

Dedication

This book is dedicated to my wife, Yvonne Nambe-Roach who has inspired me for more than forty years to strive for the best, to remember the past, and continue to act in the now.

Akil Freeman lives in
New Brunswick, New Jersey.
His favorite things to do are
exploring his town, listening to
music and playing basketball with his friends.

One day, while playing in the park, Akil noticed a group of people gathered around a large statue. Curious, Akil moved closer into the crowd to see what they were looking at. He saw a man standing in front of the statue and the man said, "This is our memorial".

The images on the memorial reminded him of pictures his father and grandfather showed him while teaching him about his ancestors on the continent of Africa.

The man said that this statue was dedicated to the memory of 137 African American men, women and children who had been kidnapped from New Brunswick and sold into slavery on a plantation in New Orleans, Louisiana. Akil immediately knew where that was. "That's the state shaped like a boot on the map."

Akil had never heard of this before and was not happy to learn that people were taken from their homes and families and forced to work for someone else.

When he went to bed that night, Akil couldn't stop thinking about what he had seen. He decided to find out more and learn about the people who had been taken. He thought to himself, "This happened to people in his town that looked just like me?"

Akil rose early the next morning and went directly to talk to his grandpa. The place to find his grandpa on Sunday morning was in the kitchen making breakfast. It is where he and his sister Maya heard wonderful stories that no one but grandpa could make come to life.

When Akil told his grandpa about his adventure, Akil could see the sparkle in his grandpa's eyes. He turned to Akil and Maya, smiled and said in a quiet voice, "children, let me tell you about our people." Grandpa sat with Akil and Maya for some time as they ate the eggs and grits that he made for breakfast. He told them stories about the strength and love of his ancestors, even though they faced many hardships.

Later that day, grandpa showed Akil pictures of their family and explained how the generations of the Freemans came to live in New Brunswick. Akil's sister, Maya, was also interested in the stories. Together, they decided to create a story about the history of African Americans in their community.

In the week following, they visited the library, talked to their neighbors, and even interviewed some of the great great grandchildren of the people who had been kidnapped from New Brunswick, New Jersey.

Akil and Maya discovered that familes kidnapped were like theirs. Even after being separated from each other they never gave up. They never forgot who they were and always remembered their love for each other. The more Akil read, the more he learned about other people who were forced into slavery. He was saddened to learn that all over the southern states black people were forced to work on plantation farms for no pay.

But finally after years of struggle, between black people in the southern states and landowners, the rich plantation owners were forced to end slavery by law.

Akil was heartened by the idea that the African American ancestors kidnapped from his community and others, never gave up on being a free people. They remained strong and determined to create homes where they could thrive.

Maya, at times, cried thinking about the struggles of slaves. But, their mom and dad always brought a smile to both of their faces when the stories of so many heroes became alive!

Dad told them it wasn't until two years later that Buffalo Soldiers and mostly black soldiers of the Union army were able to force the local landowners to end their enslavement of our people.

He told them about how rich plantation owners in Texas did not follow the law, as many enslaved people had not been told of their freedom.

Fisk Jubilee Singers

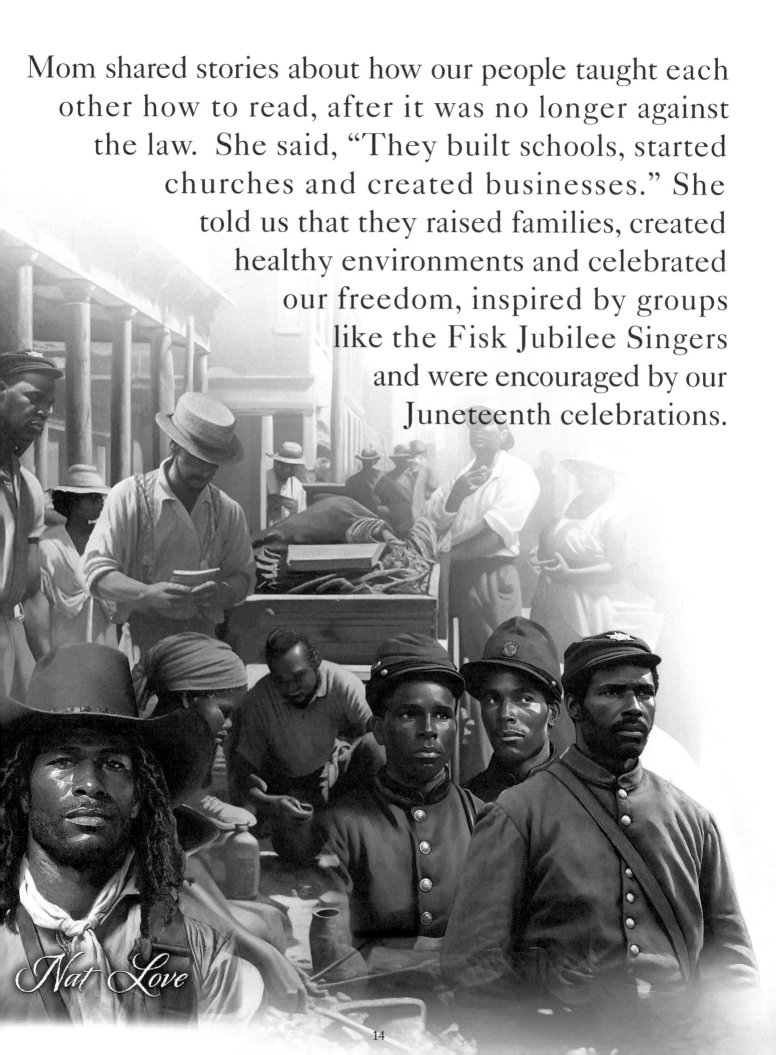

Mom shared stories about how our people taught each other how to read, after it was no longer against the law. She said, "They built schools, started churches and created businesses." She told us that they raised families, created healthy environments and celebrated our freedom, inspired by groups like the Fisk Jubilee Singers and were encouraged by our Juneteenth celebrations.

Nat Love

Akil thought the wonderful marching
bands of Historically Black Colleges
and Universities throughout the south
must have made our ancestors feel much pride.

Maya became so excited in their research after learning about HBCU's and how these colleges were soon built throughout our communities.

Their project completed, Akil and Maya shared what they had learned with their classmates, friends, and community. They felt so proud to be a part of such a powerful people.

In their classes Akil and Maya talked about the strength and resilience of their ancestors, and how they had overcome unimaginable challenges to create a better life for future generations.

Akil's mom and dad later explained to them, that the Lost Souls Public Memorial Project shared with them the importance of celebrating the strength of African American ancestry and telling all citizens about what happened. For this reason, they erected this monument in their honor. Their struggle will never be forgotten.

*This is the
Sankofa Bird.
It represents
the idea of moving
forward in life,
while learning from
the past.*

Sankofa Bird

*Its egg
in its mouth
represents our
Roots, the Past
that we have all
lived through.*

Akil is so proud to be a part of a community that has such a rich and powerful history. He and his community learned from the past and can use that knowledge to continue, to learn and grow.

Printed in the United States
by Baker & Taylor Publisher Services